A VERY HAIRY CHRISTMAS

BY SUSAN LOWELL

ILLUSTRATED BY JIM HARRIS

RIO CHICO
BOOKS FOR CHILDREN

Rio Chico, an imprint of Rio Nuevo Publishers®
P. O. Box 5250
Tucson, AZ 85703-0250
(520) 623-9558, www.rionuevo.com

Edited by Theresa Howell ~ Book design by David Jenney

Printed in China

FIRST IMPRESSION

8 7 6 5 4 3 2 1   12 13 14 15 16 17 18 19

Library of Congress Cataloging-in-Publication Data

Lowell, Susan, 1950-
 A very hairy Christmas / by Susan Lowell ; illustrated by Jim Harris.
     p. cm.
 Summary: When hungry Coyote, instead of Santa Claus, visits their desert home on Christmas Eve, three javelinas must figure out how to save Christmas.
 ISBN 978-1-933855-80-6 (alk. paper)
 [1. Christmas--Fiction. 2. Javelina--Fiction. 3. Coyote--Fiction. 4. Southwest, New--Fiction.] I. Harris, Jim, 1955- ill. II. Title.
 PZ7.L9648Ve 2012
 [E]--dc23
                         2012005769

For Nora Mary Finn

~ SUSAN LOWELL

To Brooke, artist extraordinaire

~ JIM HARRIS

Once upon a Christmas Eve,

creatures were stirring all through the house.

It was a little adobe house in the middle of a cactus forest, deep in the heart of the desert. The creatures who lived there were three little javelinas—wild, hairy, Southwestern cousins of pigs.

"*¡Feliz navidad!*" they sang as they worked. "*¡Feliz navidad!*"

"Santa's coming tonight!" said the first little javelina, whose name was Juan. He was baking gingerbread javelinas.

"Yikes!" said his brother, José. "They're SPICY!"

"Your cookies almost do backflips in my mouth," said their sister, Josefina. "What's in them?"

"My secret ingredient!" said Juan.

Meanwhile, cactus mice iced tiny cookies. Striped crickets played "Deck the Halls" while fuzzy spiders spun special holiday webs. Finally everything was ready.

With a splash of delicious colors—peppermint! orange! plum!—the desert sun went down. The wind blew icy cold.

Way off in the distance, something howled.

But indoors everyone was warm and cozy.
The crickets chirped out the Nutcracker Suite:
"TWEE-tweet-tweet-tweet-tweet-tweet . . ."
And Josefina twirled and twinkled through the
Dance of the Sugar Plum Hairy. You see,
Josefina was a prima ballerina javelina.
"*¡Olé!*" cried the audience.

"Listen!" said Juan. "Was that a howl?"

"It's just the wind," said José.

Josefina peeked outside, but all she saw was night.

"I'm sleepy," yawned José.

"Me too," said Juan.

"Me three," said Josefina.

So they filled a plate with special spicy cookies for Santa. Next, each little javelina set a cowboy boot in front of the woodstove, and they all went to bed.

The striped crickets played "Silent Night." The mice fell asleep in their nests. The spiders curled up in their webs. And then, suddenly, way out in the desert, something clattered.

The three javelinas opened their big brown eyes and twitched their hairy ears. Quick as three flashes they sprang to the window.

Bumpity-bump through the cactus came a miniature wagon and eight tiny mule deer. The javelinas couldn't see the driver, but they heard his jolly voice.

"Now, Bambi! Now, Buckeye! Now, Dusky and Dawn! On, Chico! On, Chulo! On, Dolores and Fawn!" he shouted. "Giddap! Dash away all!"

"Santa!" cried the three little javelinas.

But instead of a *swoosh*, they heard a THUNK. Chains clanked. The wagon stopped dead in its tracks.

"FLY-y-y!" yelled the voice. Now it was not jolly at all. But the tiny mule deer just shook their antlers.

Quickly the voice changed again. It sounded sweeter than a candy cane: "Fine. Take a break, my dearest little deer. Stay there and rest your tootsies. I'M going in!"

A strange shadow climbed right past the javelinas' pink snouts. Surprising sounds came down from the tin roof: "Hee! Hee! Hee! WHEE! At last!"

"He's here!" whispered Juan.

"Shh!" said Josefina. "He's magic. Stay back!"

So they peeked around the corner. The woodstove door banged open, and a cloud of ashes flew out.

"Huff! Puff!" said the cloud. "I mean—ho-ho-ho!"

He was dressed in fur from head to foot. A big white beard hid most of his face, except for his nose, which was *not* like a cherry. It was pointed.

"Where's his bag of toys?" whispered José.

"Why does he have claws?" hissed Juan.

"Santa . . . Claws?" gasped Josefina.

Place Gifts
HERE!
Thank you!

His eyes! How they twinkled when he saw those super-spicy gingerbread javelinas!

"Mmmm . . . piggies!" he chuckled.

Crrrunch! The secret ingredient exploded all over his tongue. It was. . . chile pepper!

What a noise came out of his mouth! Was it a shriek? A sneeze? A siren? No, it was all three at once.

"Hee! Ha! Ho! HO*LY jalapeños!" he screamed, and his beard flew off.

He was sly Coyote. And he was still hungry.

"Little pig, little pig," Coyote called out. "Time for din-din!"

"Not by the hair of my chinny-chin-chin!" shouted all three little javelinas.

Juan ran, José hopped, and Josefina gracefully leaped away.

"Silly Coyote," Josefina said. "We're not pigs. We're *javelinas!*"

CRASH! Down came the Christmas tree. All the mice jumped out of bed, and all the spiders stretched their legs. The crickets began to play, "Do You Hear What I Hear?"

"I think I'll eat you with red *and* green chile sauce," snarled Coyote. "For Christmas!"

"Yikes!" cried Josefina, dangling from the piñata.

Whack! The piñata shattered. Nuts and candy came tumbling down, and so did Josefina. But she landed perfectly on one tiny toe, and then Josefina began to spin . . . and spin . . . and spin. . . .

Coyote's eyes went round . . . and round . . . and round . . .

Juan tied him up with lots of ribbon. José taped his muzzle shut. Josefina held out the empty sack, and Juan and José stuffed him inside. Finally Josefina added a big shiny bow.

"I hear sleigh bells!" cried José suddenly.

"Me too!" said Juan.

"Me three!" said Josefina. "Bedtime, quick! Sleep tight, Mr. Coyote…"

They woke to a magical Christmas morning. A rare desert snowstorm had passed in the night, frosting the steep purple mountains and icing every cactus white. And playing in the snow outside they found eight new friends.

Inside, there was magic too. Everything was tidy. Every crumb of gingerbread was gone. The striped crickets were playing "We Wish You a Merry Christmas," the tree and the piñata were back in their places, and the three cowboy boots were bulging with presents.

"*¡Feliz navidad!*" said the three little javelinas.

"Happy javelinas!" shouted the eight tiny mule deer, who were invited to dinner along with everyone else.

Just before they sat down to eat, Josefina opened the last present.

"Hairy Christmas," squeaked Coyote in a sorry little voice.

"Hairy Christmas!" said Juan and José. But with their mouths full, it sounded more like "Harruh Kustmat."

"A very Hairy Christmas to all,"

said Josefina Javelina.
Standing on tiptoe under the
desert mistletoe, she gave Coyote a
very hairy kiss.
Coyote said, "Ooh!"

And if you'd just been kissed by the
Sugar Plum Hairy, you'd say "Ooh!" too!